Cuddle Bear's BOOK of HUGS

Claire Freedman   Gavin Scott

Kane Miller
A DIVISION OF EDC PUBLISHING

Cuddle Bear LOVES giving hugs,
And cuddles when he can,
But one bear can't hug everyone,
So here's his **clever** plan.

HUG ACADEMY

"A school for little bears!" he cheers.
"My **Hug Academy**!
I teach them all my cuddling skills.
Come, peek inside and see!"

"In cuddle class," says Cuddle Bear,
"We learn what **hugs** can do.
They **cheer** you up! They make you **smile**,
When you've been feeling **blue**!"

Then Cuddle Bear calls,
"Practice time!

Now, find a
partner, please!

Let's keep it light,
don't hug too **tight** -

A **cuddle**,
not a **squeeze!**"

The bears must all keep **fit** and **strong**;

They work out in the **gym**.

And even **whales** might need a **hug**,
So each bear learns to **swim**.

They practice on an **octopus**,
To get used to the **tickles**.

And **porcupines** need special care,

Because of all their prickles!

Giraffes are **very** hard to reach,
But they **still** need a cuddle.
Frogs are small and **slippery** –
Bears could get in a **muddle**!

Whatever **size**, whatever shape,
From teeny up to **tall**,
Or growly, fluffy, bouncy, shy–
There is a hug for all.

Today at last, it's hug **exams**–
A very special day–
As each bear shows its cuddling skills,
The others cheer, "**Hooray!**"

Ready, teddy, cuddle!

"**Well done!**" says Cuddle Bear with pride,
"You **ALL** have passed the test.
You've earned a yellow heart that proves
Your cuddles are the **BEST!**"

So if **YOU** want to spread some love,
And show friends that you **care**...

...Give someone close a cuddle now,

As hugs are made to SHARE!

To Mark and Ruth with lots of love
~ C F

For Vics, Laurie and Frida
~ G S

First American Edition 2017
Kane Miller, A Division of EDC Publishing

Text copyright © Claire Freedman 2017
Illustrations copyright © Gavin Scott 2017
Published by arrangement with Little Tiger Press Ltd, London

For information contact:
Kane Miller, A Division of EDC Publishing
P. O. Box 470663
Tulsa, OK 74147-0663

www.kanemiller.com
www.edcpub.com
www.usbornebooksandmore.com

Library of Congress Control Number: 2017930983
Printed and bound in China
1 3 5 7 9 10 8 6 4 2

ISBN: 978-1-61067-669-4
LTP/1800/1806/0517